MISTRESS OF HATHI

Phillip Barea

Copyright © 2023 Phillip Barea

All rights reserved

In Loving Memory of My Father

I. THE DESERT

The morning dawned upon two travelers amid a desert wilderness. As the sun threw its powerful rays over the horizon, they flooded a plain where no boundary could be traced but the sky. There was nothing to relieve the dull and uniform sterility of the scene but the occasional trunks of a few stunted trees, which appeared to stand there only as visible records of the utter barrenness of the place. The sad wayfarers awoke from beneath the slight shade of one of those skeletons of the wilderness to pursue a journey with no prospects. They were far advanced upon a wide inhospitable desert, where no welcome oasis was to be seen, and where the fellow traveler was seldom met.

The travelers were Kayum and his wife, Aisha. They, due to a marriage not approved by their respective families, had fled from their country in the West to seek a new home and peace in the East. The man was handsome, of noble stock, possessing all the generous qualities of his people. He was bold, active, enterprising, with great endurance, and with the advantage of a mild and placable spirit. The woman was young and beautiful, but extremely delicate; especially due to her condition as she was about to become a mother.

When they arose on this sad morning, they nearly consumed the last of their provisions. They had a small quantity of water in a leather bottle, which the husband made his fainting wife drink before they proceeded on their way. To linger was certain death, and to advance seemed only a dalliance with hope; there appeared to be no chances for relief. They had several days' travelling left to perform without having been provided enough sustenance for so long and arduous a journey; and the chances of meeting other travelers were so remote as to render their perishing in the wilderness almost a certainty.

She was mounted upon a small lean horse, a pony, which for the last several days had been so sparingly fed that it could hardly continue the journey. The weakened woman was ignorant of the extent of her danger. She knew not that all of their provisions had been exhausted, save one small rice cake which the tender husband had reserved for her use. He kept from her the awful fact of their utter destitution, lest in her precarious condition it should bring on premature labor in a place where no assistance could be obtained, and she would thus probably perish. Despite the misery of their situation, he still entertained the hope that they could obtain relief. Trusting in the mercy of the God who guides the wanderer as well in the wilderness as in the populated country, he pursued the journey with a heavy and foreboding heart.

As the sun continued to rise, the heat became intolerable. There was no shelter from its scorching rays. The anxious man held an umbrella over the head of his wife as he walked painfully along by the side of her lean pony; but after a while his arm became so cramped that it was only with difficulty that he could bear the weight of the umbrella. This, though not great, was the more sensibly felt from the elevated position in which he was obliged to keep his arms. He was, however, miraculously sustained by his anxiety for the dear woman near him, who bore with unrivaled endurance privations which in her state were especially deplorable. They travelled through a long and difficult day, and the rice cake was consumed long before they halted for the night.

There being no shelter nearby, the husband fixed the handle of his umbrella into the ground, and throwing over it a thin scarf, formed a kind of rudimentary tent, under which his wife could rest without immediate exposure to the dry desert air. She was exhausted with fatigue; her tongue was parched with thirst, and the rapid increase of circulation too plainly told that a fever was fast coming on. To attempt to understand the husband's agony was a vain endeavor. Without food and without water, his wife in the pains of labor, and with no hope of relief amid a vast wilderness, which even the wild beasts shunned as a solitude where only death and desolation reigned; he had no thought but that both must lie down and die.

The sufferings of his ailing companion were appalling, yet she bore them without a murmur. The severity of her pangs aggravated that thirst by which she had been so long and so grievously oppressed. He had but one alternative, and did not hesitate to adopt it in such a trying emergency. His wife's agonies were increasing with each passing moment. He left the insecure canopy which he had erected for her temporary accommodation, seized his dagger, ran to the pony, and, in an outburst of tumultuous anxiety to save the life of the object dearest to him on earth, plunged it desperately into the animal's throat. Having caught the blood in a wooden bowl, he then took it to the tent.

During his short absence, his wife had already become a mother. The cry of the poor child raised within him, at this moment, emotions of parental joy; but these were in an instant stifled by the consciousness of those awful perils by which he was surrounded. He put the bowl to the lips of the suffering mother; she took a small drink, and was to a slight degree refreshed. He then built a fire upon the open desert, and broiled some flesh from the animal which he had just slaughtered. It was tough and rank. However, the juices of this unpalatable meal subdued to a degree the yearnings of hunger and the dreadful pangs of thirst.

In the morning, when the sun again cast its vivid light upon the vast level of the wilderness, this wretched pair agreed to pursue their journey. The husband dreaded the increased difficulties which he would have to overcome. His companion was so weak that she could barely stand; yet she was obliged to carry her infant, as he was loaded with their baggage and other necessities that had previously been confined to the back of the pony.

They had scarcely embarked upon the continuation of their melancholy journey, when they were encouraged by the prospect of relief. Not more than half a mile distance before them, a beautiful lake seemed to smile in the morning sun, and invited the suffering travelers to bathe their limbs in its cool waters. The margin was dotted with groups of trees, displaying a luxuriant foliage, which was reflected in the still mirror below, and promised a graceful shade to the weary traveler.

Beyond this oasis, a gorgeous city displayed its battlements amid the solemn silence of the desert, over which it seemed to cast the glow of its splendor. It spoke with a mute but eloquent voice to the heart of the forlorn wanderer, for they alone can appreciate its magic who have braved the perils of the wilderness, and seen death stand before them face to face amid its vast and inhospitable solitudes.

Kayum and Aisha, overjoyed at the sight, made the best of their way towards the lake and the city, in which the stir of busy life seemed to prevail. They saw, as they imagined, multitudes of their fellow humans exit from its gates and spread over the adjoining plain. The scene, to the excited imagination of the travelers, was animated beyond description.

The sight of human habitations, and of human beings who could afford them aid; of water in which they might quell the pangs of the most painful of bodily privations; of houses in which they might find shelter after their perilous journey; all gave such a stimulus to their exertions, that even the weak and suffering mother, with the assistance of her husband's arm, was able to go onward with tolerable firmness.

When they had proceeded for some time, the lake and the city still appeared before them, but still far away. It seemed to them as if they had been moving their limbs without advancing a single step. They still pressed forward under the delusive expectation of reaching the goal of their hopes; but after a while the lake began to suddenly disappear, the city was by degrees shrouded in a mist that dispersed in the course of a few minutes, and, to their frustration, they saw nothing save the wide arid expanse of the desert before them. The unhappy woman sank upon the earth in mental agony. The miserable man was now perfectly overwhelmed with despair.

He feared that his wife was dying. She could no longer carry the infant; and there was, consequently, but one alternative. The struggle of nature was a severe one, but no choice remained between death and parental sacrifice. The desire for life prevailed; and it was determined, after an agonizing conflict, that the infant must be abandoned. The mother's tears were dried up on her burning cheeks, and the father's pangs were lost in the anxieties of a husband. The appeals of nature were only stifled by louder appeals within both their hearts; and, however fierce the repugnance, it was to be resisted and overcome.

The death of their child was the lesser of two evils; and they therefore submitted to the stern severity of their condition.

It was agreed by the weakened parents, that the newborn pledge of their affections should be abandoned. The mother, having kissed it fervently, consigned it to the arms of her husband, who, having taken it to a spot where the stunted stock of a tree protruded from the scorching sand, placed it under the scanty shade of this bare emblem of the desert. He then covered it with leaves, and left it to the mercy of that God who can protect the child in the desert as well as the sovereign on his throne.

On rejoining his wife, the man found her so weak that he feared she would be unable to proceed. Though released from the burden of her infant, her lack of strength was so extreme from the united effects of mental and bodily suffering, that she could scarcely rise from the earth. The pangs of thirst were again becoming horrible; and still, after a severe struggle, she rose, and the pair continued on their journey in silence and in agony.

They had not gone far before the invincible yearnings of parental nature prevailed over mere physical torment, and the bereaved mother called in a voice of piteous anguish for her child. She could no longer endure the pains of separation. The idea of having voluntarily consented to become the instrument of its death was a horror that increased with every step, and she sank exhausted upon the sand. The sun, now rising towards its highest summit, poured upon her the fiery effulgence of its beams. The husband's heart was subdued by her sufferings. Dashing a tear from his cheek, he undertook to return and restore their infant to the arms of its feeble mother. Fixing the handle of his umbrella again in the ground and throwing the scarf over it, he placed his wife under that frail covering, and immediately retraced his steps.

With a sad heart he reached the spot where he had deposited the infant; but to his surprise the leaves were removed, and a black snake was coiled around it, with its hideous mouth opposed to that of his child! In a frenzy of desperation, he rushed forward; but was instantly arrested by the instinct of paternal fear as he stood before the objects at once of his tenderest interest and of his terror, as if he had been suddenly converted into stone. The previous motion, however, had evidently alarmed the monster; for it gradually uncoiled itself from its victim without committing the slightest injury, and retired into the hollow trunk from whence it came.

The father snatched up his child, and carried it in ecstasy to its mother; but she was outstretched under the scarf in the last struggles of life. Her weak spirit had been overwhelmed by her lengthened sufferings of mind and body, and she now rested at the point of death. She raised her eyes languidly, received the babe with a faint smile upon her face, and tenderly kissed it. The effort overcame her, and she fainted. After a short time, she rallied; but it was only to die. The husband hung over her with mute but intense tenderness, and cursing in his heart with bitterness those relatives who had caused the death of all he valued upon the earth, and had rendered him the most desolate of men.

"Kayum," said the dying woman, "dig me a grave in the wilderness; don't leave this poor body to the birds of prey. We shall be reunited with each other. There is a paradise beyond this world where all the good people meet and are blessed, and we shall be among them. I die happy in your love, and in the knowledge of never having forfeited my claim to it."

Kayum could not speak. He pressed the love of his life to that heart which she had so fondly inhabited, and scalding tears of agony flowed down his cheeks. He threw his arms tenderly round her, his heart throbbing painfully, and buried his bursting face into the hot sand beside her. She spoke not, she stirred not; he raised his head to kiss her fading lips, and those lips were slightly parted, but fixed; a faint smile was on her cheek, yet no breath came. She was dead.

II. DEATH AND LIFE

Kayum raised himself from the earth, turned his eyes with a look of reproach towards heaven, and succumbed to a burst of sorrow. Then, bringing the strong energies of his mind to resistance, the anger quickly subsided, and he bowed to his fortune with the fortitude of a man who looks upon endurance as his province, and upon calamity as his lot. During the whole of this melancholy day, he did not leave the body.

His wife's dying request was in his ears and in his memory, "Dig me a grave in the wilderness", and he resolved to comply with it.

He passed twelve lingering hours in a broiling sun, occasionally laying himself under the scarf beside the corpse, close to which his infant child slept unconscious of its loss. His thirst became at length so excessive that his throat and tongue swelled, and he began to feel suffocated. His face was blistered and sore, his eyes were inflamed from the combined effects of weeping and the glare of the sun upon the white sands of the desert. Towards the evening he was so overcome by his sufferings that he laid himself down to die. The infant cried for food, but he had none to give it. Taking the linen shirt from his body, which was saturated with sweat, he put it to the child's mouth, and this kept it alive.

Kayum's tongue had by this time enlarged to such an immense size that he could not move it. The inflammation was so great that he was unable to close his lips. Expecting death at any moment, he pressed still closer to his breast the innocent child, when he was unexpectedly relieved by the cracking of sores in his mouth. A copious discharge of blood followed, which passed into his stomach, and somewhat soothed the fever that burned inside him. He was so relieved by this effort of nature, that he almost immediately sank into a short but refreshing sleep.

The sun had gone down in brightness; and when he awoke, the stars were looking upon him from their thrones of light, and smiling above him in their beauty. The intensely calm darkness of the sky seemed an emblem of the rest that dwells there. A gentle breeze had broken the oppressive stagnation of the air, and fanned his hot, blistered features as with an angel's wing. His energies revived. Though the thirst by which he was still parched affected him greatly, it was to some degree mitigated by that balmy breath of heaven, which he felt now for the first time since he had entered the desert.

He commenced his melancholy task of digging a grave to enclose the remains of a person who had been dearer to him than his own life. He took his dagger and began to remove the sand. It was an arduous and sorrowful task. After an earnest application of mind and body for two hours, he succeeded in creating a hole four feet deep. Into this he tenderly lowered the body of his departed wife, filled up the pit, and throwing himself upon it, laid there until morning.

Towards dawn he fell into a deep and death-like sleep. He was at length woken up by feeling himself severely shaken. Upon looking up, he perceived himself to be surrounded by strangers. They were travelers on their way to Aman, capital city of the Hathi Empire. They gave him food and water; and the infant was fed with goat's milk by means of a sponge. His strength being now somewhat revived, he joined the travelers, and advanced with them to their destination.

Aman was the perfect place in which his talents soon displayed themselves. Kayum was no ordinary man. He soon attracted the notice of Emperor Shahdab, who had a singular ability for discovering talent, and from that moment he rose to distinction. Shahdab perceived his value, and made use of it to promote the interests of his empire. Kayum advanced by a regular but rapid progression until he became high treasurer of the state. He was a chief political organ of one of the wisest sovereigns that history celebrates, and was held in high regard by the whole nation. The emperor placed implicit confidence in him, it was well deserved, and it ended only with his death.

The daughter of Kayum, who had been so providentially preserved in the desert, was honored with the name Damira, meaning heart. As she grew up, she excelled in personal beauty and attributes over all of the loveliest women of the empire. The extraordinary event which had distinguished her birth seemed but as the prognostication of future distinction, and the child of the desert grew to be the perfect woman.

The greatest care was taken to make her mistress of every accomplishment available that could grant additional value to the natural graces of her sex. In vivacity, wit, spirit, and the appetite for knowledge, she was unrivalled by few and surpassed by none. In vigor of understanding she stood alone and unapproached. Her beauty was the theme of universal praise.

Suitors from all quarters sought her hand; but it was not easily won. Prince Yash of Bayana, a proud noble of distinction, at length presented himself; and to him she was betrothed. Imperial historians speak of Prince Yash as the most eminent person of his age, and much esteemed by the emperor, who never failed to bestow his favor upon brave men. He was of lofty stature, and no less remarkable for the handsomeness of his form and features than for the rare qualities of his mind. He was universally acknowledged to be in every way worthy of the beautiful Damira, by whose preference he felt equally flattered and delighted.

Soon after she had been betrothed to Yash, the lovely Damira was seen by Prince Reyansh, later known as Emperor Reyansh, who became so desperately in love with her, that imagining there could be no obstacle to her union with a prince of the blood, he applied to his father Shahdab, for his consent to marry the beautiful daughter of the high treasurer, Lord Kayum.

The emperor sternly refused his consent; at the same time chastising his son for seeking to degrade himself by way of a low alliance. Prince Reyansh was destroyed; and, to his mortification, the accomplished Damira soon after became the wife of Yash.

Reyansh was from that moment the implacable foe of his successful rival. He could not bear to hear his hated name mentioned in his presence, and, with cowardly vindictiveness, was set upon his destruction. He kept these feelings a secret from his father, who esteemed Yash too highly to approve of the prince's hostility towards him, and had, moreover, expressed his satisfaction at the latter's marriage with Damira.

Reyansh, however, secretly fomented jealousies among the other nobles against the popular imperial favorite. These men were easily excited; for it would never be hard to find persons ready to go against those to whom they are conscious of being inferior in moral excellence; and especially in royal courts where ambition is the ruling passion. Nothing can be less difficult than to provoke the envy of people whose sole aim is aggrandizement, and who are therefore naturally predisposed to think poorly of any other who happens to contravene those aims, or to cross the path of their ambition. The prince, therefore, had little difficulty in accomplishing his purpose. He secretly disseminated gossip to the injury of Yash, who in disgust retired from the court to his palace in the provincial city of Bayana.

III. THE TIGER

Their life in Bayana was relatively simple and full of affection; and although the local custom was to keep wives in a separate and isolated set of living quarters, a harem, the couple endeavored to spend time together. They were only expected to have conjugal relations but once a week, and even then, just to have sex for the purpose of procreation. But the happy couple slept together on most nights, such was the fire of their passionate romance.

In the assigned conjugal bedroom, decorated with flowers and fragrant with perfumes, Yash would receive Damira, who always came bathed and appropriately dressed, and he would invite her to eat and drink freely. He would then sit her beside him, and holding her hair in one hand he would gently embrace her with his other arm. They would then carry on with amusing conversations on various subjects, and eventually talk suggestively of love and lovemaking, all while caressing each other. At last, when they were overcome with desire, they would proceed to a lovingly aggressive exercise of passionate affection.

In the aftermath, the lovers would sit on the terrace of the palace and enjoy the moonlight, and carry on in conversation. For example, while she sat on his lap, with her face towards the moon, she would show him the different planets, the morning star, the polar star, and the seven Rishis, or Great Bear.

After a short time in Bayana, Damira became pregnant and would later give birth to a daughter whom they named Aisha, after Damira's mother.

There they lived undisturbed for several years until the death of Emperor Shahdab, which caused a period of sincere mourning by the whole nation, who in the death of their emperor deplored the loss of a great and good man. When Prince Reyansh became sovereign, his passion for the daughter of Kayum revived with full force. The restraint being removed under which the smothered flame had been so long and so painfully suppressed, it burst forth with increased fierceness.

He was now absolute; and being determined to possess the object of his frustrated love, he made advances towards a reconciliation with Yash. But the brave prince for a time resisted all his pleadings, perceiving their purpose, and resolving to part neither with his wife nor with his honor, as he could not resign the one without relinquishing the other. His strength was remarkable, and his bravery equal to his strength; his integrity was unimpeached, his reputation high, and he was alike feared and respected by all. Upon every occasion where danger was imminent, he was foremost to encounter it; and thus, his valor was the theme of many a romance and of many a song.

His bodily vigor was so great, that he had once slain a lion singlehanded; from which circumstance he obtained the nickname the Lion Slayer, Prince Yash the Lion Slayer. He was, however, also esteemed for his virtues as well as for his bravery; and Damira fully appreciated his rare endowments. She was proud of his reputation. To her, the emperor's feelings were no secret; but she avoided his presence in obedience to the wishes of her husband, who was not altogether without his suspicions that the hostility which the new sovereign manifested towards him was solely on her account. He continued, therefore, in his provincial seat without visiting the imperial capital.

Not long after Reyansh had ascended to the throne of Hathi, Yash was invited to court, and after repeated solicitations, he accepted the invitation trusting to his own high reputation for security against any tyrannical exercise of the sovereign power. Upon his arrival he was carefully handled by the emperor to lull suspicion. Open and generous himself, he suspected no treachery in others. He left his wife at Bayana, not willing to expose her to the chance of attention from the sovereign, who might keep alive former predilections, and therefore renew his criminal hostility.

The young emperor's court was splendid to the extreme. He was fond of formal state functions; but hunting being his passion, a day was appointed for the chase. All the chief nobles of the empire attended, hoping to have an opportunity of exhibiting before their royal master their skill and prowess in a pursuit extremely dangerous in eastern countries. A vast train, swelling to the number of an army, went forth from the gates of Aman. Upwards of five hundred elephants, upon which rode the emperor and his court, led the retinue towards a jungle where the quarry was expected to be roused. The howdah (an elaborate seat for riding on the back of an elephant) of the royal elephant was covered by a silk canopy, and its whole framework was skillfully ornamented with precious metals. Thousands of spears glittered in the sun, the rays of which were reflected in streams of glowing light from those various arms borne by this motley cavalcade. The neighing of steeds was mingled with the busy hum of men who thronged to the scene with excitement.

Yash accompanied the court on horseback, armed only with the sword with which he had slain the lion, having by that act immortalized his name in the records of his country. His royal master showed him a marked respect, occasionally consulting him respecting the chase; thus, aggravating the jealousy of the other nobles, they being already sufficiently hateful towards him. He received the emperor's courtesies with a cold but modest respect, not entirely forgetting former unkindness, though without suspicion of future injury.

The royal party at length entered the jungle, where the forest haunts of the tiger were shortly explored. The spotters soon enclosed a mighty beast, and Reyansh immediately proceeded to the spot. He began to entertain a hope that the period so long desired had arrived when he would have an opportunity of exposing the life of his rival in an encounter from which the latter would have little chance of escaping. Seeing the tiger at a short distance, surrounded by hunters, lashing the ground with its tail and giving other tokens of savage hostility, the despot demanded of those around him, who would venture to attack the ferocious beast?

All stood silent and confounded. They had not expected such a proposal: nor did they appear to entertain any wish to expose their lives in a conflict in which more danger than glory could be reaped.

As none of them advanced, and the emperor began to raise his brows and show symptoms of displeasure, Yash already entertained a hope that the enterprise would devolve upon him; but, to his extreme mortification, three nobles stepped forward and offered to encounter the forest tyrant. Reyansh cast upon the bold Yash a glance of such disappointment that his pride kindled, and he longed to show how unafraid he was to engage the beast. But as three nobles had first demanded the encounter, he could not set aside their prior claim to a distinction which they insisted upon achieving.

After receiving the approval of their royal master, they prepared for the encounter, dismounting from their elephants, and arming themselves with swords, spears, and shields. Yash, fearing that he was likely to be rivalled, and that his fame would be tarnished by inferior men undertaking a conflict which by his silence he might be supposed to have declined, advanced, presenting himself before the sovereign, and saying firmly:

"To attack an unarmed creature with weapons is neither fair nor manly; it is taking advantage of an animal which cannot plead against such injustice but by a fierce retaliation. Such is not in accordance with the character of the truly brave. All such contests should be undertaken upon equal terms. God has given limbs to us as well as to tigers, and has imparted reason to the former to counteract a deficiency of strength. Let the nobles of your imperial majesty then lay aside their arms and attack the enemy with those only with which God has provided them. If they shrink from such an encounter, I am prepared to undertake it."

Reyansh rewarded the speaker with a smile of gracious approval; but his nobles, one and all, declined such a perilous contest, insisting upon the madness of the enterprise. To the Emperor's infinite surprise and delight, the bold Prince Yash instantly cast aside his sword and shield, and prepared to engage the tiger unarmed. The circle of hunters, which had surrounded the jungle tyrant, opened to admit the champion.

The ferocious beast with which he was to engage rested at the base of a tree, snarling hideously as its enemy approached, erecting the fur upon its tail and back, passing its tongue every now and then over the terrific fangs with which its jaws were armed, but seeming ill disposed to commence the contest. Yash was stripped to his pantaloons, and his fine muscular frame, a model for an ancient god, exhibited its noble proportions as he advanced cautiously but firmly towards his enemy. The tiger rested upon its belly without attempting to stir, nevertheless giving evident tokens of a determination to retaliate if attacked. The magnificent paws projected from beneath its chest; and upon these it occasionally rested its head, until roused by the approach of its adversary.

Every eye was fixed upon the scene; and every heart throbbed with the strongest emotion of anxiety. The sovereign alone sat upon his elephant, apparently calm and undisturbed; but the deep flush upon his cheek showed that he took no ordinary interest in the approaching encounter. He did not utter a word as he saw the man whom he considered doomed to inevitable destruction march resolutely up to the prostrated tiger and strike it in the ribs with his foot. The animal, now excited to ferocious resistance, instantly sprang to its feet, but crept backward with its face to the enemy and its belly to the ground. Yash advanced as it retreated, keeping his eyes fixed upon those of the enraged beast. At length the latter suddenly turned, and bounded forward; but was stopped by the spears of the hunters, who still encircled it at a distance, and were all prepared to prevent its escape. Finding its purpose foiled, it again turned, and being beyond the influence of Yash's eye, prepared to make its ferocious attack.

Yash now retreated in his turn, and, pausing near a tree, awaited the approach of his enemy. It instantly bounded onward, sweeping its tail above the ground with an uncertain motion, but without uttering a sound. The brave champion, who from experience was well acquainted with the habits of such animals, knew that the creature was about to spring forwards. Placing his right foot forward, and planting his left firmly against the projecting root of the tree, he calmly awaited the pending attack. The tiger crouched, and uttered a short sharp growl, projected its body forward with a speed and force which nothing could have resisted; but the prince leaped aside as the living projectile was about to fall upon him, and turning quickly, seized his baffled foe by the tail. He then swung it around with a strength and dexterity that astonished every beholder, brought its head into such violent contact with the tree, that for several seconds it was completely stunned.

After a while, however, it recovered, but lay still and panting, not at all relishing, as it seemed, a renewal of the conflict. As the victory was not yet decided, Yash again approached the prostrated beast to rouse it to resistance. He kicked it several times, but it only growled, lashed its tail, showed its fangs and remained perfectly passive under these acts of aggression.

The hero, tired of this indecisive mode of warfare, seized it again by the tail, and, swinging it round as he had already done, brought its head once more in stunning contact with the tree. The blow, though severe, did not produce the same effect as before; for the enraged animal, suddenly rising to the full height of its stature, turned on its aggressor with a savage roar, and seized him by the flesh behind his thigh. As his pantaloons were loose, the tiger was somewhat deceived, and therefore, did not take so large a mouthful as it no doubt would have done had the limb been entirely naked. Yash instantly grasped it by the windpipe, and, squeezing it with all his might, soon obliged the creature to relinquish its hold; but with a violent twist it freed itself from the strong grip of its adversary, and instantly renewed the encounter.

The struggle now became indeed terrific, and the anxiety of the spectators increased in proportion to it. Reyansh could no longer control the feelings by which he was overcome. His parted lips, between which his tongue protruded with a quivering nervousness of motion, his eyelids raised as to show the entire sphere of his eager, restless eyes, the tremulous aspect of his whole frame showed the extent of his interest in the issue of this unnatural struggle.

By this time the tiger had again rallied, and having raised itself upon its hindlegs, struck both its forepaws upon the prince's chest, tearing the flesh from the bone. Yash fell under the weight of this deadly assault; but, still undismayed, after a desperate effort he contrived to roll over upon his panting foe, now nearly exhausted from its exertions and by the severe blows it had received, and, forcing his hand in between its extended jaws, griped it so firmly by the root of the tongue, that in a few seconds it laid strangled beneath his grasp. He then rose streaming with blood, pointed to his dead enemy, made a salute to the emperor, and left the field grievously injured. The emperor was astonished by the entire display.

The champion was then transported home in a stretcher, and for several weeks his life hung in the balance. To the surprise of Reyansh, Yash eventually recovered, though he carried the marks of the tiger's claws to his grave. The royal rival was nevertheless determined not to forego his purpose of destroying this remarkable man, though he feared to do it openly.

Meanwhile, the hero continued to move about, everywhere unattended, utterly unsuspicious of a plan against his life. He was not conscious of having offended a human creature, and therefore did not suppose that any person living could desire his death. He lived at ease; but whenever he appeared at court, which he occasionally did, he was always treated by the sovereign with marked respect and great apparent cordiality. This, however, was only to mask the bloodiest intentions, which were no secret to many of the nobles, who, in common with their master, desired the destruction of a brave man because he was a hated rival.

Eventually, private orders had been given to the jockey of a large elephant to waylay the prince and trample him to death. The opportunity did not immediately occur, as the victim travelled at uncertain times; and although his movements were watched, it was found a difficult matter to come upon him at a favorable moment. One day, however, as he was returning from the public baths on a palankeen (a covered litter for one passenger) through a narrow street, observing an elephant approaching, he ordered his palankeen-bearers to turn aside and permit it to pass. As the huge animal came near, he observed that there was no room for it to pass without crushing the palankeen, and thus endangering the lives of himself and his attendants.

The elephant still came charging. Yash called out to the rider to stop, but his order was disregarded.

The jockey sitting upon its neck, apparently in a state of half consciousness, took no heed of the danger to the party before him. Yash, seeing that it was impossible to avoid the approaching danger except by making a timely retreat, ordered his bearers to turn and carry him back to the baths; but they, terrified at the evident hazard to which they were exposed, threw down the palankeen and fled, leaving their master to settle the question of priority of right of way on the emperor's road. The hero, undismayed by the formidable size of the jeopardy by which he was menaced, sprang instantly from the ground, drew his sword, and before the elephant could accomplish its fatal purpose, severed its trunk close to the root. The gigantic animal immediately dropped and expired. The rider had already leaped from its neck as it was in the act of falling, and escaped.

Yash, suspecting that in urging the elephant upon him the fellow had been motivated by that personal feeling which generally exists between different classes of people, decided not to pursue him, thinking the simple passions of a hireling too contemptible to rouse his indignation. He therefore allowed the offender to escape unmolested, and coolly wiping the blade of his sword, returned it to the scabbard.

Reyansh witnessed the whole scene, as he had

placed himself behind a small lattice window that overlooked the street. He was perfectly amazed, but disappointment and vexation eliminated from his heart any better feelings. Yash later visited him and communicated what had occurred; and the emperor extolled his bravery with warmth, and thus escaped his suspicion.

IV. SUCCESS AND CAPTIVITY

Repeated disappointments only served to increase the sovereign's jealousy. It raged like a furnace within him; for to exercise due control over their actions is not the general character of despots. His peace of mind was perpetually disturbed by the fierceness of his emotions, and he became more than ever bent upon the death of his successful rival for the affections of Princess Damira.

Yash was not permitted to remain unmolested for long. Sardar, a royal governor, knowing his master's wishes, and to ensure his future favor, hired forty assassins to murder Prince Yash. So confident was the latter in his own strength and valor, that he took no precautions to protect himself against neither secret nor open enemies. When in Aman, he lived in a solitary house in which he retained only an aged porter, all his other servants occupying apartments at a distance. Relying upon his own courage and the vigor of his arm, he had no fear of either the secret assassin or the open foe.

This was a tempting opportunity. The murderers were prepared, and had been promised such a reward as would encourage them to engage in the most desperate exertions to ensure the fulfillment of their employers' wishes. They entered the apartment while their victim was asleep. A lamp hung from the ceiling and threw its dim light upon him as he reclined in a profound slumber. There was no mistaking the hero, as he lay with his noble head upon his arm, and his expansive forehead turned towards the light, every line blended into one smooth unbroken surface denoting the perfect peaceful rest. Over his muscular frame a thin sheet was lightly thrown, which did not entirely conceal his handsome proportions, and exhibited the indistinct but traceable outline of the figure beneath. He slept profoundly.

The murderers approached the bed and raised their daggers to strike; when one of them, touched with remorse at the idea of such a cowardly assault upon a man who had so famously shown his courage and virtues, cried out, under the impulse of an awakened conscience:

"Hold! Are we men? Forty to one and we are afraid to encounter him awake?"

This timely interposition of the assassin's remorse saved the life of his intended victim. Yash, aroused by the expostulation, jumped from his bed, seized his sword, and retiring backwards before the assassins had all entered, reached the corner of the apartment where he prepared to defend himself to the last. As he retreated, he had drawn the couch before him, thus preventing the immediate contact of his enemies, who endeavored in vain to reach him; and as they were only armed with daggers, he cut down several of them without receiving a single wound.

Urged on, however, by the great amount of the reward offered, the murderers still pressed upon him, and succeeded at length in dragging the couch from his grasp, though not before he had caused several others to pay for their temerity with their lives. He was at length exposed to the full operation of their brutal fury. Ten of his enemies already lay dead on the floor, showing fatal evidence of the strength and speed of his arm. There, however, remained thirty to vanquish; and, placing his back against the wall, the hero prepared for the unequal and deadly struggle.

Seeing him now entirely exposed to their assault, the ruffians rushed simultaneously forward, in the hope of being able to dispatch him at once with their daggers; but they so encumbered each other by suddenly crowding upon their victim that they could not strike. He then, taking advantage of the confusion, laid several of them dead at his feet. Nevertheless, they pressed forward, and the same result followed. Shifting his ground, but still managing to keep his back against the wall, he defeated all of their advances; and such was his fearful precision in employing his sword, that not a man came within its sweep without receiving practical experience of the strength with which it was wielded. Besides those already slain, many others of the assailants fell desperately wounded. At length the rest, fearing the extermination of their whole band, fled and left him without a wound.

The man who had warned Yash of the danger stood fixed in mute astonishment at the prowess of him whom he had received a commission to murder. He had been so paralyzed that he could neither join in the attack nor defend his victim from the sanguinary assault which the latter had so heroically defeated. He had no time for meditation. The charge had been so sudden, and the defense so marvelous, that his mind remained in a state of stagnation, and was restored to its proper function only upon seeing the extraordinary survivor.

Perceiving himself to be alone with the man whom

he had undertaken to destroy for a cheap bribe, his heart sank within him and he felt that he deserved to die; but his intended victim advanced, and kindly taking his hand, welcomed him as his deliverer. Having ascertained from the man's reluctant confession by whom the assassins had been hired, the hero dismissed him with a liberal pardon.

This remarkable exploit was subsequently repeated from mouth to mouth with a thousand exaggerations; so that wherever Prince Yash appeared, he was followed and pointed to as a man of superhuman powers. Songs and romances were written to extol his prowess and magnanimity. He was cheered by the populace wherever he approached. Mothers held up their babies to behold this extraordinary warrior, blessing him as he passed, and praying that their sons might emulate his virtues. He was flattered by these popular votes in his favor; nevertheless, to avoid a recurrence of perils like those from which he had so recently escaped, he retired to Bayana.

Meanwhile, the Emperor, burning with secret rage at hearing the valor of his rival be the theme of every tongue, gave orders to his creature, Sardar, to seek a more favorable opportunity than he had before availed himself, to destroy this detested noble, for such was his astonishing strength and dexterity, that Sardar dared not attack him openly.

Being now at a distance from court, the bold prince thought himself beyond the influence of his sovereign's jealousy, and, with the natural frankness of his character, immediately cast aside all suspicion of mischief. Sardar, coming with a great retinue to Bayana with the pretense of making a tour of the territory placed under his political superintendence, communicated to his officers his secret mission. They heard him with silent pleasure; for most of the nobles, being jealous of a rival's popularity, with a mean and dastardly spirit joined readily in the scheme for his destruction.

Unsuspicious of any hostile intention towards him, the devoted prince went out to meet Sardar as he was entering the town, and the latter affected to treat him with great cordiality. He rode by the governor's elephant, familiarly conversing with the nobles who formed his entourage, and frequently receiving a gracious smile of approval from the emperor's viceregent. He was completely thrown off his guard by this apparently courteous bearing; and abandoning himself to the generous warmth of his nature, invited the nobles to his palace, with the intention to entertain them with a feast equal to the liberality of his disposition; a determination which he knew his wife, the beautiful Damira, would not be amiss in fulfilling.

In the progress of the cavalcade, a pikeman, pretending that Yash was in the way, rudely struck his horse. In a moment the latter's suspicions were aroused; his face darkened, and he cast around him a look of fiery indignation. Without an instant's delay he drew his sword and clove the offender to the earth. Knowing that no soldier would have thus acted without orders, the insulted noble immediately saw that his life was aimed at, and directly spurring his horse towards the elephant of the treacherous Sardar, he tore down the howdah, seized the cowardly man by the throat, and buried his sword in the traitor's body before any of his guards could rescue him; then turning upon the other nobles, five were almost instantly sacrificed to his just revenge.

Covered with their blood, the avenger stood before them, sternly braving the retribution which he saw them preparing to inflict, and hailing them with a loud defiance. He expected no quarter, and therefore was determined not to yield without a struggle. His mind was braced with the extreme tension of desperate energy, and he decided that the coveted prize of his death should be dearly won.

Those who were within the immediate reach of his arm he slew without distinction, and such was the fatal velocity of his motions that the enemy fled before him in dismay. He did not pursue, but like a grim lion, he stood defiant before them, spotted with the gore of the slain, and prepared for fresh slaughter, but there was not an enemy daring enough to approach him.

Terrified at his prowess, the soldiers began to discharge their arrows at him from a distance. His horse, struck in the forehead, fell dead underneath him. Then springing onto his feet, he slew several of the enemy who had ventured to rush forward in the hope of dispatching him while encumbered with the corpse of his fallen steed. They fled at the sight of their slain comrades, and left their unvanquished destroyer to the aim of his distant enemies, who fired upon him without intermission. Covered with wounds and bleeding at every pore, the still undaunted lion slayer called upon Sardar's officers to advance and meet him in single combat, but they one and all declined the encounter. They saw that certain death to each of them would be the result of such a contest. It was evident, moreover, that their victim could not escape the aim of so many arrows.

At length, seeing his end approaching, the brave prince, as a man of faith, turned his face towards the heavens, then prostrated and threw some dust upon his head by way of ablution. Then standing up, calm and undismayed, before the armed ranks of his murderers, he received at once six arrows in his body, and expired without a groan.

Thus perished one of the greatest heroes whose exploits have had a conspicuous place in the history of nations.

The beautiful widow and her daughter were captured and immediately transported to Aman, but Reyansh refused to see them, whether from remorse or policy is uncertain. He ordered that they be confined to one of the worst apartments of his harem, and this was exceedingly galling to Damira's sensitive and haughty spirit.

The harem of a ruler is a central political and social sanctuary, from which emanate all the cabals and conspiracies so rife within the cabinets of potentates. It may, therefore, be appropriate to give a brief description of a sovereign's domestic arrangements.

In the harem are educated the royal princes and the principal youth among the nobles that destined for posts of responsibility within the empire. It is generally separate from the main palace, but so close as to be of ready access. None are admitted within its apartments except for the emperor and those immediately attached to its several offices, the duties of which are performed by women. It is generally enclosed by high walls, surrounded by spacious gardens, and laid out with all the splendor of eastern magnificence, where every luxury is obtained that the appetite may demand or money can procure.

Those inmates who form the matrimonial confederacy of the potentate are among the most beautiful women that the empire can provide. They are taught embroidery, music, and dancing by older women hired to instruct them in every blandishment that may captivate the senses and stimulate the passions. These lovely captives are never permitted to appear outside except when the emperor travels, and even then, they are conveyed in litters enclosed by curtains, or in boats with small cabins, the windows admitting the light and air only through narrow Venetian blinds.

The apartments of a harem are splendid, always, however, in proportion to the wealth of the prince. The favorite object of his affections exhibits the dignity and enjoys the privilege of a queen, though a queen in captivity. While her beauty lasts, she is frequently regarded with a feeling almost amounting to idolatry, but when that beauty passes away the warmth of love subsides, her person no longer charms, her voice ceases to impart delight, and her faded cheeks and sharpened tones become disagreeable memorials of the past.

The favorite, however, while she continues her dominion over the heart of her lord, is treated with sovereign respect throughout the harem. She smokes her golden-tubed hookah, the mouthpiece studded with gems; and enjoys the fresh morning breeze under a veranda that overlooks the gardens of the palace, attended to by her damsels, who are themselves only second to her in attractiveness of person and splendor of attire.

Here she reclines in oblivious repose upon a rich embroidered carpet from the most celebrated looms of the world. Through an atmosphere of the richest incense, she breathes the choicest perfumes, and has everything around her that can minister to sensual delight; still, she is generally an unhappy being. She dwells amid splendid misery and ungratifying profusion, while all within herself is desolation and hopelessness. Her sympathies are either warped or stifled; her heart is blighted and her mind degraded. She cannot join in the enthusiasm of the poets, but languishes, as the seasons turn, in the most debasing captivity, and feels that the breeze breathes not upon her either the freshness of freedom or of joy.

V. IMPERIAL LADY

The daughter of Kayum was a woman of an arrogant spirit, and could not accept the indifference with which she was treated by her former admirer. It preyed deeply upon her mind. She was not ignorant of the emperor's hostility towards her late husband, though she seemed unconscious to the fact that it had been the cause of his death. She severely felt her bereavement; and the change from perfect freedom to captivity, from the affection of a generous husband to the indifference of a capricious master, deeply mortified her. Meanwhile, however, she was not idle; the resources of her mind were no less fertile and extraordinary.

Being an expert at working with tapestries and all kinds of embroidery, and in painting silks with the richest patterns and colors, she applied herself with great devotion to those employments. Through intense application, she acquired an expertise that enabled her to transcend the works of the best manufacturers in the empire. In a short time, the exquisite products of her taste and skill became the talk of the capital, and she immediately became a person of importance, apart from her being the widow of the renowned Prince Yash. The ladies of the nobles of Aman would wear nothing upon grand occasions but what came from the hands of the lovely Damira; she was consequently soon pronounced the oracle of fashion and of good taste.

While she affected an extreme simplicity in her own dress, she attired her attendants in the richest scarfs and brocades, making those who had attractive persons the vehicles for setting off to an advantage the works of her own industry. She thus amassed a considerable sum of money, and became more celebrated in her obscurity than she had hitherto been as the wife of the most distinguished hero of his age. Her milder glories until then had been eclipsed by the predominancy of his.

Notwithstanding the success of her exertions in the occupation to which she had devoted herself, Damira was still an unhappy woman. She loathed her captivity; and she deeply felt the moral degradation to which she was subjected, and that the influence which she imagined herself born to exercise was extinguished by an untoward destiny. She had always entertained a secret conviction that the strange events of her birth prophesied a mortal distinction of singular splendor; it therefore mortified her to find that she continued to live celebrated only as a fabricator of brocades and scarfs.

Her spirits drooped, and she grew peevish and irritable. Her occupation became a toil and she talked of relinquishing it, when one day she was told that there was an old woman in the harem who was able to look into the future and read the destinies of people. Damira immediately sent for the prophetess. The crone appeared before her while bending beneath the weight of her years. Upon seeing the widow of the late Yash, she lifted her skinny arms, clasped her bony fingers together, and muttered a few incoherent words which seemed more like madness than of prophecy. There was in fact, however, more sanity than madness in the mummery, it was a sort of label for her gift of fortune telling.

"Well, mother," inquired Damira mildly, "what do those strange words portend? I would know something of my destiny, if it is in thy power to read it; if not, take this, and leave a blessing behind thee; for an aged woman's curse is a dreadful thing to hang over anyone's head."

Saying this, she placed a gold coin upon the woman's right palm, who giving a chuckle of delight, mumbled forth her prediction with a distorted grin of satisfaction.

"You were born in a desert to die upon a throne. She who as a babe was embraced by a reptile, as a woman will be embraced by a king. The infant that was brought into the world amidst famine will go out of it amidst plenty. The star, so puny at thy birth, will expand into a sun. I am not deceived; believe me, and leave here a proof of your faith." She extended her hand, and having received another golden reward, retired.

Damira was willing to believe the prophecy of the witch. There was something in it, despite its vague generalities, that harmonized closely with those silent beliefs which she had for some time past permitted herself to cherish. She was ambitious, and a thirst for distinction was her ruling passion. Her mind was too strongly fortified against superstition to render her the dupe of a juggler's predictions; nevertheless, the mere promise of aggrandizement was agreeable to her ear, and she therefore lent willing attention to what her reason despised, but not caring to pay for the indulgence a thousand times above its value.

She cherished the promise of worldly exaltation, not because she believed the hag who made it had a greater insight into the future than her neighbors, but only because the theme was agreeable to her sensitive ambition; and there moreover existed a strong feeling within her, that she should rise from the groveling condition to which she was now reduced, and be exalted in proportion to her present degradation.

Motivated by this feeling, she did everything in her power to give currency to her reputation. She knew well that her taste was the theme of general approval, and the marvelous power of her beauty began to be talked of beyond the confines of the harem. A noble of distinction, holding a high office in the state, offered her his hand, and it was soon rumored that she was about to become his wife. She secretly encouraged this report, though she had given him no pledge, hoping that it would come to higher ears and procure for her an interview with the emperor.

This state of things could not last long; and when pressed by the impatient noble for a definitive answer to his offer of marriage, to his astonishment and that of all who were acquainted with the situation, she declined it. Mortified by this refusal, he was determined to obtain by force what was denied to him, and he took an opportunity of violating the sanctity of the harem by appearing before her. She was alone in her apartment when the disappointed lover entered. He commenced by chastising her for her deceit, which she bore with dignified patience, until, irritated by her calmness, the man seized her arm and roused her indignation with the most offensive menaces. She was as an infant in his grasp; nevertheless, with the impulse of aroused passion, she suddenly burst from his embrace, rushed into an inner chamber, and, seizing a dagger, commanded the intruder to retire.

Maddened by disappointment, he sprang forward to repeat the violence which he had already offered, and she instantly raised her arm and buried the dagger into his body. He fell covered in his own blood. He was then taken from the apartment insensible; and sentenced to a confinement of three months to his bed. This taught him a lesson never to pass from memory but with his life. Despite this episode, other suitors sought her hand, and all with equal success.

The accomplishments of this singular woman were soon carried to the ears of the emperor, who had probably by this time forgotten the dominion which she once held over his heart; or perhaps it was that the mortification of her having been the wife of another rendered him sullen in his determination not to see her. He resolved, however, now to visit her, to have ocular proof of whether the voice of public opinion was truth or exaggeration.

One evening, therefore, he proceeded in earnest to her apartment. At the sight of her unrivalled beauty, all of his former passions revived in an instant. She was reclining on a sofa in a thin robe of plain white muslin, which exhibited her faultless shape to the best advantage, and became her better than the richest brocades or the finest embroideries. As soon as the emperor entered, the siren rose with an agitation that served only to heighten her charms, and fixed her eyes upon the ground with polite confusion. Reyansh stood mute with amazement, and rapture took immediate possession of his soul. He felt, if he did not utter, the sentiment of an eminent poet. He was dazzled by the perfection of her form, the dignity of her posture, and the transcendent loveliness of her features.

Advancing to where she stood with downcast eyes and flushed cheeks, blushing in the dazzling fullness of her beauty, he took her hand and said:

"Empress of women, the emperor of a great and mighty nation throws himself at thy feet as an act of just homage to thy beauty. Wilt thou be the Queen of Reyansh the Mighty?"

"A subject has no voice," replied the enchantress; "and a woman especially can have no will but that of her sovereign. It is his privilege to command and her heritage is to obey."

Reyansh again took her hand, declared his resolution to make her his empress, and immediately a proclamation was issued for the celebration of the royal nuptials with the lovely widow of the late Prince Yash.

A general festival was observed throughout the empire. Those rich embroideries which had lately been the admiration of the ladies of Aman no longer issued from the harem. The humble seamstress cast aside the distaff for the crown, and in time she proved to be one of the most extraordinary women which the pen of history has celebrated. She became the principal director of the complex machine of government.

From this moment she was acknowledged as the favorite wife of the Emperor of Hathi. As a distinguishing mark of her preeminence in the sovereign's affections, she was allowed to assume the title of Empress. Her family was held next in rank to the Princes of the Blood, and advanced to places of the highest trust. Its members were admitted to privileges which had never been enjoyed by subjects not of the bloodline under the empire's dominion. The coin of the realm was stamped with her name, as well as with that of the sovereign. She converted the harem into a court, where the mysteries of state policy were discussed with a freedom and a power seldom known under despotic governments.

It was from the harem that celebrated decrees were issued; and, although they passed in the emperor's name, it is credibly believed that they emanated from his empress. This rendered the reign of Reyansh one of the most politically prosperous in the annals of history. Her influence exceeded that of any other person in the empire, even the sovereign. Perhaps, it could be said that under the rigid implementation of traditional policy in Hathi regarding women sharing in the administration of the state, there never has been an instance of a woman attaining an ascendence so paramount, and such perfect political control over the destinies of so many subject principalities as the renowned Empress Damira.

VI. REBELLION

Some years after the elevation of this extraordinary woman, Taksh, the second son of Reyansh, who later would himself ascend to the imperial throne, began to disrupt the harmony of the state. He had been sent with a powerful army into the south to quell a formidable confederacy against the empire, and having succeeded in reducing the insurgents to obedience, began to show his ambitious desire for the crown. Under the most plausible of pretenses, and while in command of the army with which he had just quelled a dangerous insurrection, he persuaded the emperor to put into his hands Kiaan, Reyansh's eldest son, and consequently heir to the throne, who had himself been imprisoned for rebellion. It soon became evident why he had been so persistent in controlling the person of his rebellious brother. Kiaan was the grand obstacle between him and the crown. The traitor Taksh now quickly threw off his mask, and publicly declared his intentions towards the throne. His success in the south had endeared him to his troops; his courage had gained their confidence, and his liberalism secured their affections. Confident in his imagined power, he disregarded the mandates of his father, continued in arms, and ordering that his unhappy brother be executed, Taksh immediately assumed the imperial titles.

The empress had long suspected Taksh's intentions. Despite the veil which he had thrown over his intrigues, they did not escape her attention. Ambition was the dominant feeling in the heart of this crafty prince. The empress, seeing the evils likely to accrue from this fierce passion if suffered to operate unchecked, was determined to take precautions to contravene his actions. Before the death of Kiaan, she saw that Taksh, into whose power he had fallen, had a plan to seize the throne. Every action of his public life had shown a secret but undeviating perseverance in the pursuit of dominion that could not to be mistaken. His cunning she felt might be overreached, but his talents were formidable. He was not only a crafty intriguer, but a brave and successful general. He had become the idol of the army; and with such a mighty engine to power, she dreaded the final success of his schemes.

She presented her suspicions to the emperor, who was at first unwilling to entertain them; but the wife had such an influence over the mind of her royal husband, that he always listened with great confidence to her suggestions. She assured him that Taksh must be watched, advised his recall, and that the army should be placed under a less dangerous command. She insisted upon speedy and decisive measures to remove the danger to the state.

To the emperor's doubts of Taksh's ambitious intentions, she answered:

"A man does not seek the instruments of authority but to employ them. When princes actively seek popularity, they intend to make the mob their tools, and the citizens their steppingstones to power. He who has once deceived is never to be trusted; and I am all too confident that, under the smiles of allegiance which so frequently play upon the features of Prince Taksh in his father's presence, hypocrisy lurks like the serpent in a bed of flowers."

After a while Reyansh was convinced by the empress' arguments regarding his son's evil plans, which an account of Kiaan's death soon confirmed. He was enraged at such a sanguinary act of ambition, and was determined to punish the fratricide

To remove the stigma that he knew would be attached to the crime of murdering a brother, the crafty prince affected such extreme grief, that he was believed by many to be innocent of so atrocious an offence. Reyansh, however, or rather his empress, was not to be deceived by this boldfaced hypocrisy. The former wrote him a letter accusing him of the crime; at the same time ordering that the body of his murdered son be disinterred. It was then brought to the capital, and buried with the honors due to his rank.

Although Prince Taksh was married to a niece of Empress Damira, the hostility between him and the empress had risen to such a height that it was perfectly implacable. The rebellious prince knew well that he owed the indignation of his father to her influence; and he therefore decided to lose no time in endeavoring to get her under his control. Seeing no probability of a reconciliation with his father, he was determined to continue with his rebellion.

At the suggestion of his consort, Reyansh prepared to reduce his son to obedience; but his troops being at a distance, he could not bring an army to the field. At this critical juncture, a courier arrived from Lord Aamod, the imperial general, stating that he was advancing, with all available forces, to join the royal army. Shortly thereafter, Reyansh's troops engaged the rebels and defeated them. The defeated prince was so overcome by this unexpected reversal of fortune, that he contemplated suicide. The feeling, however, passed, and he fled to the mountains, where he found for the moment a secure refuge from the anger of his father and the hostility of Damira.

Misfortune followed him and his party was defeated in another battle. Still, the royal rebel was so formidable that it was agreed to take him alive as the only means of extinguishing the flames of civil war, which was always disastrous to the victors as well as to the vanquished. Aamod was therefore dispatched, at the head of a large detachment of Bactrians, a race of soldiers proverbially brave, to capture the royal insurgent. Taksh, as a consequence, halted his retreat, determined to face the danger and take the chance of another battle. Crossing a nearby river he threw up mud walls to defend his position along the banks.

Of the large and well-equipped army that had followed him into the south there remained only a small dispirited remnant, and desertions were thinning his lines every day. He could not rely upon the soldiers, who were dejected from successive defeats, and murmuring for their arrears of pay, which he was unable to provide. He lost his energy, became incautious and irresolute, and allowed himself to be surprised by the imperial general, who routed his disheartened forces with a great slaughter, and forced him again to seek refuge in the hills.

His escape was a source of severe mortification to the empress, who foresaw that the peace of the state was not likely to be secured until he should either be taken or destroyed. She was also anxious that the succession should be fixed upon Aarush, the third son of Reyansh, who had married Aisha, the daughter that she had with Yash. With her suggestions, no doubt just, the emperor's enmity towards his son was kept alive; of which the latter being aware, saw that it would not be prudent to trust himself within the walls of his father's capital. He had more than once thought of throwing himself at the mercy of paternal love; but his knowledge of the empress' vindictive spirit, and the consciousness of his own manifold derelictions, kept him from running the risk of captivity for life, if not of undergoing extreme punishment.

His affairs, however, now began to assume a more favorable aspect. Having captured the fort of Tellum, on the eastern edge of the empire, and with a new army which he had raised in that province, after an obstinate defense by the garrison, he then succeeded in taking the surrounding area by storm. This unexpected success animated him to new exertions. He now overran the whole district, which shortly submitted to his might. He conquered Dhakar, a considerable city, and once the capital of the province, in which he found an immense treasure of gold and silver, as well as jewels and weapons. The ruling prince was deposed, and a new governor assigned, who ruled in the name of Emperor Taksh, through which title the prince finally declared his claim to the imperial throne.

No sooner had he settled the new government, than he turned his thoughts to the neighboring province of Azar. The governor fled at his approach; but the wealthy nobles crowded to his camp to offer him their allegiance. He accepted their submission, together with the rich presents which they brought to ratify the mutual compact of protection and affinity, and to confirm their sincerity. But the most important occurrence, and which greatly tended to strengthen him in his new conquests, was the unexpected submission of Jarak, governor of the fort of Hoda, who came to his camp, presented him with the keys, and made a vow of perpetual fealty. This fortress was considered impregnable. It had never been taken by force, and was therefore looked upon by the rebellious prince as a place of security for his family. He immediately moved them there; and being now relieved from anxiety on their account, he was better prepared to encounter the dangers of the field, and to brave the vicissitudes of fortune.

This uninterrupted current of success inflamed the pride of the royal rebel, and he fancied himself in a condition to contend for the imperial scepter with that army which had already twice so skillfully defeated him. Aamod had again taken to the field, and marched as far as Sodagar to chastise the insurgents, who had mustered upwards of forty thousand horses, a force only slightly inferior to the imperialists in number, and were drawn up on the bank of a small stream.

The battle was desperate but decisive, with the rebels being routed after a monstrous slaughter. The conduct of Prince Taksh on this occasion was marked by reckless bravery. Plunging into the thickest of the fight with five hundred horses, who had pledged to devote themselves to death with their leader, he maintained a bloody struggle against immense odds, and would, no doubt, have fallen a victim to his own despair, had not some of his officers seized the reins of his horse, and forced him from the battle to a place of safety. He then fled to the fort of Hoda, where he had left his family. The plunder of his camp, which contained the spoils of Dhakar, saved him from immediate pursuit.

Leaving his family in the fortress, where he

imagined they would be secure, the wretched prince collected the scattered remnants of his army, and threw himself into the city of Kanwal, which he was later determined to defend, but thought it prudent to evacuate at the approach of his enemies. He then fled towards the south. The provinces which he had so lately conquered quickly fell again under the legitimate authority of Hathi. After Aamod had reestablished the government of these districts, he marched against the royal fugitive.

Though his fortunes were reduced to so low an ebb, the prince did not despair. His mind was active, and these severe reverses only seemed to animate him to new enterprises. He attached to his desperate fortunes the Prince of Omur, who entertained some cause of enmity towards Reyansh. Strengthened by the forces of this new ally, he conquered the city of Amuran; but when the imperial army arrived, it forced him to flee the siege and take shelter in the nearby mountains. In his retreat he made an attempt upon a strong fortress on the frontier, where he was repulsed with a considerable loss.

This completed his ruin. His nobles no longer followed him; and the troops, under the sanction of their example, deserted his standard. Only a thousand horses remained. His spirits sank within him; his misfortunes oppressed him; and his guilt and folly were always present in his mind. Sickness was also added to his other miseries. He was hunted like a wild beast from place to place; and all humankind were his enemies.

Where he thought he could not overcome, he fled; and he spread devastation to places where he could prevail. He was, however, by this time tired of fighting. Worn down by contention and hostility, he wrote letters of compunction to his father wherein he enlarged his own guilt, and he even added, if possible, to his own wretchedness and misfortune. Reyansh was often full of affection and he was always weak. He was shocked at the miserable condition of a son whom he had once loved; and his tears fell upon the part of that son's letter which mentioned guilt, and his crimes vanished from memory. Amid this returning softness, Reyansh was not altogether forgetful of policy. He wrote to his son that if he would give orders to the governors of Hoda, Dhakar, and other places which were still held in his name, to deliver up their forts and send his three sons to court, he would be forgiven for his past crimes.

Taksh embraced the offer with joy; he delivered up the forts and sent his children to Aman. He himself, however, found various pretenses for not appearing in person at court. He alleged that he was ashamed to see a father whom he had injured so much; but in truth he was afraid of the machinations of the empress. He made excursions, under a pretense of pleasure, to all parts of the empire while attended to by five hundred horses. Such was the termination of this formidable rebellion, the suppression of which Reyansh entirely owed to the vigilance and foresight of his empress, Damira. This remarkable woman was ever conspicuous amid the great stir of the times; and in every action of her life, she displayed that predominance of mind that had distinguished her even before her exaltation to the imperial scepter, which she may be said to have wielded; for though it appeared to be in the hand of her husband, she gave strength to the grasp by which he held it, and imparted stability to his throne.

VII. JUDGEMENT

Among the extraordinary occurrences of Damira's life, perhaps there is none that more forcibly develops her character than her bearing towards Aamod after the services which he had rendered to the state by suppressing the rebellion of Prince Taksh. The eminent abilities displayed by Aamod during his command of the imperial armies had already won for him the confidence of his master and of the empress; and this confidence was increased by his suppression of the most formidable rebellion which had blemished the reign of Reyansh. His relatives were raised to offices of trust in the government, and the emperor treated him with a distinction that excited the envy of the nobles. But the gratitude of princes has ever been a questionable virtue; for their suspicions are readily excited.

The empress soon became apprehensive of Aamod's influence with the emperor; and therefore, to restrain it, put into operation the active energies of her mind. Reyansh was naturally a credulous man, but the rebellion of his son had already made him suspicious. The virtues of his general ought to have placed him above the petty surmises suggested by envy; but his abilities had created for him enemies at court, and his master lacked the firmness to repel the insinuations levelled against the man who had been the main prop of his throne.

Aamod soon perceived a change in his sovereign's feelings; but, aware of his own integrity, he was at no pains to remove the prejudices excited against him. He was conscious that he owed much of the growing coldness in the emperor's manner towards him to the misrepresentations of Damira; and there grew a strong and mutual antipathy that nearly proved to be the means of transferring the empire from the current bloodline to another dynasty.

The immediate cause of the open rupture that ensued, and had nearly cost Reyansh his crown, was an accusation made to the empress by another noble that Aamod had sanctioned his son's death, which the father expressed himself determined to avenge. He further stated that the general entertained a plan of raising another of one his sovereign's sons to the throne. This was reported to the emperor and it immediately stoked his fears, and he listened with weak credulity to a charge of treason against his general. Blinded by his terror, he forgot the services which that great and good man had rendered to the state, and weakly listened to the voice of his slanderers.

Aamod, who was at this time touring the fringes of the empire, received his master's imperative orders to return immediately to the capital. As he did not instantly obey, he received a second summons, still more peremptory, accompanied with such manifestations of displeasure that he could no longer mistake the danger of his situation. Although surprised at this total change of good feeling towards him, and yet having really done nothing to justify his sovereign's displeasure, he was resolved to obey the mandate at all hazards, but to also take every necessary precaution against his enemies.

When, however, he reflected more upon the unworthy requital he had received for his services, indignation and disgust overruled his first resolution, and he came to the determination of retiring to a castle of which he had some time before been appointed governor. But, to his astonishment, he found out that an order had been received at the fortress to deliver it into the hands of a person whom the empress had appointed. This unjustifiable act of tyranny convinced him of what some of his friends at court had already told him, that his life was in danger from the secret machinations of his enemies; and he decided therefore not to put himself in their power before he had at least made some effort to ascertain the extent of his peril.

He wrote to the emperor, expressing surprise at his hostility towards an unoffending subject, and declaring that, though he had the greatest confidence in the honor of his sovereign, he had none in that of his evil counsellors. The only reply which he received to this temperate declaration was an order, still more peremptory than those already sent, to appear at court without further delay. To refuse was to rebel; and he therefore addressed another letter to his imperial master.

In it he said: "I will serve my sovereign with my life against his enemies; but I will not expose it to the malice of his friends. Assure me of safety, and I will clear myself in your presence."

This letter was construed by the empress, who directed all of the emperor's affairs, as an insult. Reyansh was angry, and dispatched a messenger, summoning Aamod, in reproachful terms, to appear before him. The general prepared to obey; but took the precaution of going with an escort of five thousand Bactrians in the imperial pay, who had long served under him, and were devoted to their commander. With this guard of faithful soldiers, he proceeded towards Aman.

When the empress heard that Aamod was advancing with so numerous an escort, she became alarmed. She feared that such a formidable force might either terrify the emperor into a reconciliation, or place his crown in jeopardy. Either way there was cause for apprehension. She persuaded him, therefore, not to admit the general into the camp, for at this time the imperial retinue was on its way from Aman to Anjool.

When he arrived near the royal encampment, a messenger was dispatched to inform him that he would not be allowed to enter the presence of his sovereign until he had accounted for the revenues of the east, and the plunder taken at the battles. Provoked by such a demand, the general dispatched his son-in-law to complain of the indignity; but no sooner had the young man entered the emperor's presence, than he was stripped, beaten, covered with a ragged robe, placed upon a lean donkey with his face towards the tail, and thus sent back to his father-in-law amid the jeers of the whole army. This was an insult not to be forgiven.

Aamod was grieved at the emperor's weakness, but attributed the scandal of the last scene to the empress, to whose intrigues he imputed her royal husband's violent hostility. He saw that to put himself in her power was at once to relinquish his liberty, if not his life; and he accordingly formed his decision. It was no less decisive than bold. He resolved immediately to surprise the sovereign and carry him off.

The imperial army was encamped on the banks of a river, across which was a bridge. On the morning after the mistreatment of Aamod's messenger, they proceeded on their march. Not being in an enemy's country, no precautions were taken against surprises and no danger was apprehended. The army commenced its march early in the morning; and Reyansh, being in no haste to move, continued in his tent, intending to follow at his convenience. When the imperial troops had crossed the bridge, Aamod, advancing with his Bactrians, set it on fire, and thus cut off the sovereign's retreat. He then rushed forward to the royal tent. His face was pale, but his whole aspect severe and resolute; there was no mistaking the purpose which was legibly written in every feature. He was followed by his brave men. Resistance was vain, and the guards and nobles were instantly disarmed.

Reyansh had retired to the bathing tent and Aamod sought him there. The guards attempted to oppose the latter's entrance; but putting his hand upon his sword, and pointing to his numerous followers, no further opposition was made, and the bold general entered the bathing tent. The nobles present, seeing the folly of resistance, relinquished their arms and became silent spectators. Aamod passed by them with a stern look, which brought to their memories the outrage of the preceding day, but did not utter a word.

Meanwhile, information of what had happened was carried to the inner tent, where the emperor was, by some of the female attendants. He seized his sword, but was soon brought to a sense of his defenseless position. Perceiving that all his guards and nobles were disarmed, and that Aamod was accompanied by a band of resolute followers prepared to obey his commands to the letter, he approached the general, whom his conscience now told him he had treated with ingratitude, and said:

"What does this mean, Aamod?"

Aamod, touching the ground, and then his forehead, thus replied:

"Forced by the machinations of my enemies, who plot against my life, I throw myself under the protection of my sovereign."

"You are safe," answered the emperor, "but what about those who stand armed behind you?"

"They demand full security," answered Aamod, "for me and my family; and without it they will not retire."

"I understand you," said Reyansh, "name your terms, and they shall be granted. But you do me an injustice, Aamod. I did not plot against your life; I knew your services, though I was offended at your seeming disobedience of my commands. Be assured of my protection; I shall forget the conduct which necessity has imposed upon you."

Aamod did not reply, but, ordering a horse, requested that the emperor mount it. They then rode forward, surrounded by Bactrians. When they had proceeded beyond the outskirts of the camp, the imperial captive was respectfully asked to place himself upon an elephant to avoid accidentally causing any confusion that might ensue from his departure. He readily complied with the general's request, seeing that opposition would be fruitless, and he ascended the elephant, upon which three Bactrians immediately placed themselves as guards. Some of the nobles, seeing the captivity of their sovereign, advanced to oppose his progress, and were instantly cut down by the followers of Aamod. There was no further interruption offered, and Reyansh was taken to Aamod's tent.

Here the latter explained himself to his royal prisoner, assuring him that he had no plan either against his life or his power.

"But," he continued sternly, "I am determined to be secure from treachery."

Aamod was greatly disappointed that he had not been able to secure the empress. During the confusion caused by the entrance of his numerous followers into the imperial tent, she had managed to escape, and passing across the stream upon her elephant, had joined the imperial army, to whom she communicated the disaster of her husband's captivity.

Aamod, not considering himself secure while the empress was at large, decided to leave nothing untried to get her under his control. He had now publicly shown his hostility; the banner of rebellion was raised, and no alternative remained but to pursue his purpose with the same resolute boldness with which he had begun it. He was conscious of the resources of his own genius. He was the idol of the troops that he commanded; and though aware of the consummate abilities of the empress, who in fact directed the movements of the imperial army and of her brother-in-law, Rahnumai the Vizier (imperial prime minister), he knew they were not popular with the troops, and that, moreover, a great number of the nobles were dissatisfied with the influence exercised by her and her family.

Aamod, having returned with the emperor to his camp on the banks of the river, found that Anush, a noble of high reputation, had just arrived to join the imperial army. Finding the camp deserted, and the emperor a prisoner in the hands of his rebellious general, Anush cursed the latter with treachery in the presence of his Bactrians. The general, at once enraged and alarmed, ordered his troops to fall upon the arrogant noble, whom they immediately slew, together with his whole entourage. This decisive stroke of severity terrified the other nobles there present, who had been watching for an opportunity to rescue their sovereign, and they fled across the river, carrying to the imperial army the melancholy news of Anush's death.

This information produced a general gloom. The captivity of the emperor excited the indignation of the empress, and of Rahnumai. Damira summoned the nobles who had just joined the army; and shamed them for their cowardice in not risking their lives in defense of their royal master. A council was promptly summoned, and a consultation held as to the best method to be pursued for rescuing the sovereign out of his enemy's hands. There was no time to be lost and the moment was critical; delay only diminished the chances of success, as it strengthened the power of the rebel, who was himself universally popular.

It was decided that they should cross the river at dawn, and attack Aamod. Reyansh, whom they had contrived to inform of this intention, began to fear for his life. He immediately sent a messenger to the vizier and ordered him to desist; but that minister, not considering himself bound to comply with the commands of a captive monarch, was determined to persevere in his intention.

VIII. BATTLE OF WILLS

At daybreak the vizier went forth with the army. Upon reaching the bridge, and finding that it had been burned down, he came to the decision of wading across the river; but the water was unexpectedly deep, and in this attempt, many were drowned. At the same time, the banks on the opposite side were so steep, that those who got there had to contend with a fierce enemy under a great disadvantage. The enemy, too, were vigilant and active, and cut them off as fast as they left the water.

Nothing could withstand the headlong valor of the Bactrians. Not a man escaped; the moment he reached the bank, he was killed while attempting to climb up it. The imperial army, however, was numerous, and the rear pressing upon the front, many at length made good their footing; but it was only to encounter enemies whose principle of warfare was to vanquish or to die. The action continued for several hours, and the slaughter of the imperial forces was astounding. The vizier did all in his power to encourage the troops, but to no purpose and they were disheartened; but still, trusting in their numbers, they continued the struggle under the greatest of disadvantages.

Empress Damira witnessed the whole scene from the riverbank, and she was greatly alarmed at beholding the slaughter of the royal forces. Her resolute spirit was roused, and her determination kindled. Mounted upon an elephant she plunged fearlessly into the stream. The empress was followed by several nobles, who, ashamed at beholding the courage of a woman, followed her into the river, and made for the other side. Urging her elephant to the middle of the channel, she waved a scarf to encourage the vizier's troops. Undaunted at the carnage before her, she stood in the howdah, and discharged her arrows with fatal aim at the enemy.

Three nobles were successively killed; yet she maintained her position, and having exhausted her quiver, demanded that another be brought to her. Her elephant was wounded three times, and her situation became extremely dangerous from the violent plunges of the animal under the excitement of suffering. Still, she continued to discharge her arrows with fearless determination.

She urged her elephant forward to the bank, soon exhausted another quiver of arrows, and called for a fresh supply. The sight of her heroism gave a jolt to the wavering courage of her brother-in-law's troops, and many effected their landing.

The battle now became sanguinary to the extreme; but the imperialists gained no ground. Despite the empress' presence, they could not overcome the determined resistance of the Bactrians. Nevertheless, they fought with a bravery worthy of better success. Damira, having urged her elephant close to the bank, allowed a Bactrian to give it a severe wound with his sword, just at the root of the trunk.

With a shrill cry the huge animal fell; but whilst it was in the act of falling, the empress had placed an arrow in the string of her bow, and shot it into the brain of her enemy, who rolled dead upon the plain. When the elephant finally fell, both empress and jockey were thrown into the stream, and, as the current was powerful, their lives were in jeopardy. But the empress, seizing her bow with her teeth, swam towards some nobles, who were crossing to second her heroic exertions. She was able to overcome the current, and with difficulty reached an elephant, upon which a noble was seated, and he rescued her from the river. But, while she was still in the water, an arrow struck her in the side; but it passed around the rib, and thus did not enter her body.

Undismayed by the danger she had just escaped, the empress continued to discharge her arrows at the enemy, doing considerable damage with her single arm. Aamod was the chief object of her aim; but he was too far from the bank to enable her to accomplish her fatal purpose. Her danger was also becoming every moment more imminent; but she continued to urge her elephant forward, reckless of personal consequences.

She had already exhausted three quivers of arrows, when a fourth was brought to her. At the first discharge she struck a soldier in the body, who instantly tore out the shaft from his flesh, and with a fierce resolution of revenge leaped into the stream. He held his sword above the water with one hand, and dashed with the other towards the empress' elephant. Already was his arm raised to strike; but before he could accomplish his purpose, another arrow from the heroine's bow was buried in his breast, and he fell.

Several Bactrians now rushed into the river to seize the empress. They soon surrounded her; but she shot her arrows so vigorously, that several of them were wounded. The rest were, however, about to capture her and the glory of the empire was in jeopardy. A Bactrian had climbed onto the back of her elephant, and commenced a fierce struggle with the noble who accompanied his mistress. At this moment, the huge animal, having received a severe wound from behind, suddenly burst forward, making its way through the soldiers by whom it had been surrounded, and scrambled up the bank. It was immediately dispatched.

As it fell, Damira leaped from the howdah, and with a voice of stern command summoned some of the imperial troops, who were engaged in a desperate conflict with the enemy, to her rescue. They obeyed a voice which they had long been taught to consider as that of their sovereign. She was soon surrounded by friends and foes. Seizing a sword, she fought with a heroism that astonished even the Bactrians, with whom valor is a heritage. A deep saber cut on the shoulder seemed only to add stimulus to her resolve. The man who had inflicted the wound received from her arm a powerful retribution when she dashed her sword into his skull, and he was instantly prostrated among the dead.

The battle now raged with prodigious fury; but the imperialists were fast giving way. At length the empress was left fighting with unabated energy, supported by only a few soldiers. The moment was critical. Two Bactrians advanced to seize her; she saw there was not an instant to be lost, and rushing to the river's bank, turned her head upon her foes with a fierce expression of defiance, and leaped undauntedly into the torrent. The two soldiers followed, resolved to make her their prisoner or die in the attempt. Despite her wound, and with a courage that nothing could subdue, she bore up against the rapid current. But, notwithstanding all her exertions, she was carried by its force down the stream. As the soldiers were more encumbered, the body of each being protected by a thick quilted tunic, the royal fugitive gained a considerable distance from them.

That portion of the imperial army which had not yet crossed the river, watched her with intense anxiety. She rose buoyantly above the waters, and after great exertions, landed upon the opposite bank. Her pursuers were by this time close upon her. Determined not to be made a prisoner, she prepared for a desperate resistance.

One of the Bactrians, being before the other, first reached the shore. The bank was steep and just as he reached the edge, his foot slipped, and he partially fell, but clung to the roots of some wild shrubs that protruded from the earth. The opportunity was not to be lost and Damira drew a dagger from her girdle, and as the soldier was struggling to regain his footing, she struck him with all her force upon the temple (his body being protected by the quilted tunic, his face was the only part that she could successfully hit). The blow was dealt with fatal aim; and it divided the temporal artery, and the man fell back into the water, covered in his own blood.

His companion, who had been carried farther down the stream, reached the bank during this fatal struggle. Overcome by the extraordinary heroism of the empress, he approached her with a profound salute and said:

"Lady, your heroic bearing deserves a better reward than captivity. You are now within my power; but, astonished at the matchless valor you have displayed, I cannot persuade myself to make you a prisoner. Promise me safe conduct back to the army to which I belong, and you are free; refuse me, and I will plunge immediately with you into the stream, where we will both perish together."

"Soldier," replied the empress with composed dignity, "I accept your terms. I promise you safe conduct to your friends. Your behavior is noble, and demands my esteem. What reward can I offer you?"

"A Bactrian never accepts a reward from an enemy. Besides, I have no claim upon your generosity. I do not spare you because you are an empress, but because I admire the valor which you have exhibited as a woman. With women it is a rare quality, and deserves its reward. I would have felt the same towards a beggar who had displayed as much."

Damira was received by her friends with shouts of joy; and the soldier who accompanied her was then conducted to a shallow place some distance up the river, where he passed over to the army of Aamod.

Seeing their empress safe, two nobles, with their followers, crossed the stream and joined the imperialists, who were now giving way on all sides. Encouraged by this fresh accession of force, the retreating party again rallied, and the contest was maintained with renewed vigor. The Bactrians were in their turn repelled. They retreated towards the tent in which the emperor was confined. Several arrows pierced through the canvas and exposed Reyansh's life to great danger, and he was then covered with a shield by an officer of the guard.

Meanwhile, Aamod rallied his troops behind the tents and turned them upon the flank of the imperialists, who, dispirited by this fresh assault, gave way, and a general routing followed. Aamod, after a hard contest, remained master of the field, which was covered with the dead.

The vizier, seeing that all was lost, fled from

this scene of carnage, and reaching the castle of Charvi, shut himself up there with five hundred men. The castle was strong, but offered a retreat of questionable security against an army flushed with recent conquest, and commanded by the greatest general of his time. Damira herself escaped to Aman; yet her safety was anything but certain, being without troops, and with all the bravest nobles of the imperial army either slain or in captivity. Nevertheless, she handled this reversal with that indomitable resoluteness so natural to her lofty and energetic spirit.

Aamod dispatched a messenger to the vizier with assurances of safety; but the latter declined putting himself in the power of a successful rebel; upon which the incensed general sent his son with a strong detachment to conquer the castle of Charvi. He almost immediately joined this officer with his whole army, and after a feeble resistance the vizier surrendered. He was, however, treated with great civility and kindness by the conqueror, which not only confirmed his good opinion, but won his friendship.

Meanwhile the emperor forwarded a letter to his royal consort, begging her to join him, speaking in high terms of the respectful treatment he received from Aamod, and giving her assurances of a kind reception. This he wrote while also urging her to forget past causes of animosity, and lay aside all thoughts of further hostilities, so that the empire might not be involved again in the horrors of a civil war. He besought her to follow him into the northern region of the empire, to where he was then proceeding; declaring that there was no restraint placed upon his movements, but that he was allowed to direct his march wherever he thought proper.

Damira, immediately seeing the desperate condition of things, decided to comply at once with the emperor's commands, being satisfied that there was more danger in resistance. She chose the lesser of two evils, and, setting out from Aman, joined her captive husband on his march towards the north. Aamod sent a strong detachment to meet her and pay her the honors due to her rank; but she was not to be deceived by so flimsy an artifice. It was evident to her that she was surrounded by her future guards; nevertheless, she appreciated the ostensible compliment, and met the emperor with a cheerful demeanor.

She was immediately subjected to a rigorous confinement. Her tent was surrounded by troops, and she was not permitted to go outside. Aamod accused her of treason against the state, and insisted that so dangerous a criminal should be instantly put to death.

"You who are Emperor of Hathi," he said to Reyansh, "and whom we look upon as something more than human, ought to follow the example of God, who has no respect for traitors."

IX. SURVIVAL

Aamod, feeling that his future safety depended upon the death of Damira, had sent a soldier to dispatch her. The agent of destruction entered her tent after midnight, when she was plunged in a profound sleep. Her beautiful limbs were stretched upon a fine carpet, the rich colors of which glowed in the light of a lamp that burned upon a silver frame near her bed. Her fine features were relaxed into that placid expression which sleep casts over the face when no disquieting dreams disturb or excite it into muscular activity. A slow and measured breath came from her lovely bosom like incense from a sacred censer.

Her right arm, naked to the shoulder, and on which the scar of the wound she had recently received appeared still red and tender, was thrown across her breasts, showing an exquisite roundness of surface and delicacy of outline that fixed the attention of the rugged soldier. He hesitated to remove so beautiful a barrier to that bosom which his dagger was commissioned to reach. He stood over his victim in mute astonishment, and he was entranced by her beauty. The recollection of her undaunted heroism disarmed his purpose, and he dropped the instrument of death. Damira was jolted by the noise and she awoke from her slumber.

Seeing a man in the tent, she jumped from her bed, and, eyeing him with calm disdain, said:

"I apprehend your purpose; you are a murderer; and Empress Damira is not unprepared to die, even by the assassin's dagger. Strike!" she said sternly, and exposed her breasts.

The man was overcome; and he prostrated himself before her, pointed to the fallen weapon, and begged her to forgive the evil purpose with which he had entered her tent:

"I am but a humble instrument of another's will."

"Go," replied the empress with dignity, "and tell your employer that your mistress, and his, knows how to meet death when it comes, but claims from him the justice that is granted to the lowest criminal. The secret dagger is the instrument of tyranny, not of justice. I am in his power; but let him exercise that power as becomes a brave and decent man."

Aamod was not surprised, though greatly

mortified, when he found that his purpose had been thus defeated. He then sought the emperor, and insisted that he should immediately sign a warrant for the death of his empress. Reyansh knew too well the justice of the demand, the wrongs which she had heaped upon the man who made it, and his own incapacity to disobey. Not having seen the empress for some time, he had to a degree forgotten the influence of her charms; and prepared, though with reluctance, to comply with the bloody request.

When the awful announcement was made to the empress, she did not exhibit the slightest emotion:

"Imprisoned sovereigns," she said, "lose their right of life with their freedom; but permit me once more to see the emperor, and to bathe with my tears the hand that has affixed the seal to the warrant for my death."

She was aware of the influence she still possessed over the emperor; and, her request being complied with, she attired herself in a plain white dress, with the simplest drapery that showed her still lovely figure to the greatest advantage, and was thus brought before Reyansh, and in the presence of Aamod.

There was an expression of subdued sorrow upon her face, which seemed only to enhance the luster of her beauty. She advanced with a stately step, but did not utter a word; and, bending before her royal husband, took his hand and pressed it to her bosom with a silent but solemn appeal. Reyansh was deeply moved.

He burst into tears, and raising the object of his long and ardent attachment, turned to Aamod, and said in a tone of trembling earnestness:

"Will you not spare this woman?"

Aamod, himself subdued by the scene, and feeling for his sovereign's distress, replied:

"The Emperor of Hathi should never ask in vain."

Waving his hand to the guards, they instantly retired, and the empress was restored to liberty and to her station. She, however, never forgot the wrong, and was determined to avenge it. She manifested no signs of hostility, but always met the general with a cheerful look and a courteous air, through which she completely lulled his suspicions. Secure in the general estimation of the troops, and especially of his faithful Bactrians, he felt no fear for his own personal safety; and having completely won the good opinion of Reyansh by his late act of generous forbearance towards Damira, he had little apprehension for the intrigues of the latter, however she might choose to employ them.

He, however, knew not the person whom he judged so lightly. Her aims were not to be defeated but by the loss of liberty. She never lost sight of her purpose save in its accomplishment, and nothing could reconcile her to the degradation which she had been made to endure. She dedicated her time to devising schemes of vengeance. For six months she plotted so secretly, that not the least suspicion was excited in the mind of Aamod. Reyansh treated him with the open confidence of friendship, and the empress appeared to meet him at all times with amicable cordiality. This, however, was only the treacherous calm which often heralds the storm.

One morning in Aman, when the general, accompanied by a considerable retinue, went to pay his customary respects to the emperor, he was attacked at the same moment from both ends of a narrow street. He was fired at from the windows of several houses, great confusion ensued; but Aamod's followers being well armed, he put himself at their head and cut his way through the assailants. His escape was a miracle; the whole of his entourage was either wounded or slain, yet he was unhurt. The plot had been so well organized, that not a single creature was prepared for it but those persons to whom it had been communicated.

The spirit of disaffection soon spread. The guards

that surrounded the emperor were attacked by the citizens; and all, to the number of five hundred, were put to the sword. The whole city of Aman was in an uproar; and had not Aamod fled to his camp, which was pitched outside the walls, he would have fallen as a sacrifice to their fury. Enraged at their deceitfulness, he prepared to take a speedy and ample revenge. The empress, for her part, perceiving the failure of her scheme, was aware that she was in a situation of extreme peril. The citizens, in turn, terrified at the preparations which the incensed general was making to punish their deceitfulness, sent some of the principal inhabitants among them to him to seek his restraint; declaring that the tumult originated with the rabble, and offering to give up the ringleaders to his justice.

Although Aamod suspected that Damira had been the principal instrument of the attack upon his life and the massacre of his guards, he masked his resentment, and accepted the offers of submission, but made a vow never again to enter Aman.

Having punished the ringleaders, he left the following morning and took the emperor with him. As they started on their journey, Aamod suddenly decided to resign from his position, and place Reyansh again at liberty. The decision was as inexplicable as it was sudden and unexpected.

He had no wish for ruling the empire. Having punished his enemies and vindicating his own wrongs, he exacted from Reyansh oblivion of the past; then disbanding his army, and retaining only a small entourage, he left his sovereign to his freedom.

Damira, not in the least moved by this act of generosity on the part of a man whom her own intrigues had forced into rebellion, was resolved to seize the opportunity of consummating her revenge. She could not forget the indignities she had endured at the hand of Aamod; that he had once attempted against her life, obliged the emperor to sign her death warrant, and held her in odious captivity.

She demanded that her royal husband should immediately order his execution:

"A man," she said, "so daring as to seize the person of his sovereign is a dangerous subject. The luster of royalty must be diminished in the eyes of the people, while he who has dragged his prince from the throne is permitted to kneel before it with feigned allegiance."

Reyansh, remembering the provocations which Aamod had received, and his temperate use of power, was shocked at the empress' vindictiveness, and commanded her, in a severe tone, to be silent.

Although she made no reply, she did not abandon her resentment. Shortly afterwards, an attempt being made upon the general's life, he found it necessary to leave his camp secretly. The emissaries of the empress were sent to capture him, but he managed to escape. He who had so lately had a victorious army at his command was now a fugitive, without a follower, and obliged to flee for his life. He had left all of his wealth behind him, which was seized by the implacable Damira; and she issued a proclamation to all the provinces of the empire, denouncing him as a rebel, commanded him to be seized, and set a price upon his head.

This violence on the part of the empress was disapproved of by both the emperor and the vizier, the latter of whom did not forget the courtesy shown to him by the fugitive after the defeat of the imperial army, when he was made a prisoner by that very man who was now pursued with such hostility by a vindictive enemy who owed him her life and liberty.

Rahnumai, Damira's brother-in-law, understood the value of Aamod. He knew him to be the best general of his time, an ardent lover of his country, and that he had been forced into rebellion by acts of repeated and unjustifiable aggression. He felt assured that such was not a man to be cast off from the state without doing it an injury that could never be repaired. Besides, he feared the lengths to which the empress' ambition might carry her, and considered that it was high time that it should be checked. Although Aamod was a wanderer and a refugee under a pronouncement of death, he held up against his reverses with the same magnanimity which had marked him when at the summit of his power.

The vizier, having found the means to assure him of his friendship, convinced Aamod to mount his horse and ride four hundred miles without a single follower, to meet and confer with that high functionary; trusting his bare and secret promise of protection. The minister was at that time encamped on the road between Aman and Bayana. Aamod entered the camp in a beggar's habit, late in the evening, placed himself in the passage that led from the apartments of the vizier to the harem, and told the eunuch that he wished to see that minister. The fugitive was immediately led into the latter's presence.

When Rahnumai saw the wretched condition of Aamod, he fell upon his knees and wept. Retiring with him to a secret apartment, the general declared his determination, notwithstanding the low ebb of his fortunes, to raise Taksh to the imperial throne. Rahnumai was overjoyed at this declaration, as that prince was allied to him by the double tie of friendship and a family connection.

The result of this conference was a general declaration, in favor of Reyansh's son, who had previously rebelled; but the emperor dying a few months later, the state was freed from the probable effects of a civil war, and Emperor Taksh ascended to the imperial throne as the legitimate heir.

From that moment onwards the empress retired from the world, devoting the rest of her days to study and the quiet enjoyments of harem life. Since her power ceased with the death of Reyansh, her haughty spirit could not accept the public mortification of seeing herself holding a secondary rank within the empire. She never again spoke of state affairs, nor did she allow the subject to be mentioned in her presence. Beyond that; the singular beauty of her person continued almost to the last moment of her life, nor was the structure of her mind less impressive.

Damira was a woman of remarkable abilities. She rendered herself absolute in a government in which women were held to be both incapable and unworthy of holding the slightest share. It was not merely by the permissive weakness of Reyansh that she acquired such a political dominance within the state; but by the superiority of her own mental endowments, and the indomitable energy of her character, before which the inferior mind and spirit of her royal husband shrank in comparison.

The End

EMPRESS

My queen
Empress mine
Beauty seen
Soul I find

Your grace
Noble heart
Body and face
Finest art

Voice commands
Humble I obey
Scent demands
Grateful I stay

Jewels shed
Toss the crown
In castle bed
Lay us down

World of ours
Yours entire
Building towers
Passions fire

Move me
Shake me
Love me
Take me

I the same
Vow to do
In your name
And for you

Build together
You and me
Until forever
Nation of we

ABOUT THE AUTHOR

Phillip is the author of several novels and poetry books, including the Chronicles of Eis series and Sidamo.

Born in Virginia; Phillip grew up in Puerto Rico as the youngest son of a bilingual and bi-cultural family. After many years of travel, study, and work abroad; Phillip finally settled down in the Atlanta area (his mother's hometown and his father's college home).

His background in international affairs and international law, as well as his nonprofit and academic work experience, greatly influenced the development of his personal philosophy.

Made in the USA
Middletown, DE
09 September 2023